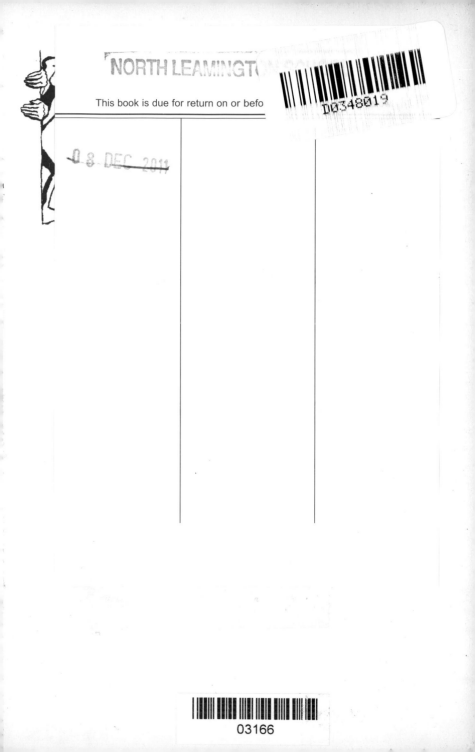

First published in 2004 in Great Britain by
Barrington Stoke Ltd
18 Walker St, Edinburgh EH3 7LP

www.barringtonstoke.co.uk

Reprinted 2004 (twice), 2005, 2006, 2007

ISBN: 978-1-84299-151-0

Printed in Great Britain by Bell & Bain Ltd

# A Note from the Author

When I was 13 I got a new, short haircut. My mum hated it so I knew it was good. She said I looked like someone who threw bottles at football matches! Next I bought some trendy clothes. They were so expensive. In fact, they used up all my savings. But I was a teenager and had to look cool.

But what if one boy decided he wouldn't waste a penny on trying to look cool? Instead, he would be an (Un)teenager ...

That's what Spencer does in *Diary of an (Un)teenager*.

I had great fun researching him. I went into schools and chatted with pupils about what they liked about being a teenager. And what they most hated.

Then I also read parts of the story aloud. I was so nervous about doing that. In fact, my throat felt very dry. But I wanted the story to feel as real as possible. So teenagers' comments were extremely important. I also wanted it to make you laugh. So, here's hoping ...

# Contents

# Chapter 1
# A Terrible Shock

**Friday, May 29th**

Strange things have started happening. I feel the need to write these important events down in a diary.

Zac rang me this evening, dear diary. He said, "Hi, Spencer! When you see me tonight you may get a shock!"

He wouldn't say anymore.

He was upstairs when I went round to his house.

I opened the door to his bedroom and then stepped back in horror.

I'd never expected this.

I blinked. But Zac was still there – and wearing ... a blue shirt that looked huge on him, the baggiest white trousers I'd ever seen and massive trainers with a huge flap and no laces.

"Why on earth are you dressed like that?" I gasped.

Zac swallowed hard, then announced, "Because, Spencer, I'm a skater now."

"But you haven't even got a skateboard."

"Not yet, I haven't," he agreed. "But I'm getting one next week. And you don't really need a skateboard these days. You've just got to have the right gear."

Then he put on this top with a hood.

"Once you've got your hoodie, you're a skater. It's as simple as that."

He smiled at me. I tried to smile back but I just couldn't.

"So how much did all this gear cost you?" I asked. "And have you still got the receipt?"

Zac whispered the price to me. I nearly passed out with shock. He'd used up all his birthday money on this rubbish. And nearly half of all his savings too.

I just couldn't believe it.

Zac and I had never wasted any of our money on clothes before. We'd been fine wearing the same shirt and jeans for years.

So what had happened to him?

"Just why have you decided to be a skater?" I asked, finding it hard to control my voice.

Zac started pacing around his room. He sighed heavily.

"It's ever since I turned 13. It's made me think about my life." His voice rose. "I've got to be something. My cousin Phil's a goth," Zac made a face, "so I didn't want to be one of those ..." He paused, then he added, "Did I tell you my cousin's got himself a girlfriend?"

"Only 700 times."

"Well, when girls see my new look," said Zac, "they might start showing me some interest. One or two might even want to go out with me."

Suddenly I started to laugh. I just couldn't help it. It was the shock of it all, really.

Then Zac hissed, "Shut up, you doughnut."

Such strong language calmed us both down.

Then he said, "You'll be 13 in a few weeks, won't you, Spencer?"

"Yes," I agreed.

"Well, you wait.  You'll start changing just like me."

Zac was staring at me now.

"No, I won't," I cried.

He smiled.

"Oh, yes you will.  You can't help yourself."

A shudder ran right through me.

Will I soon start throwing all my money away on stupid clothes?

No, dear diary, I won't.

I am going to stay EXACTLY as I am now.

And that's a promise, signed here in my diary.

# Chapter 2
# Hitting the Youth Club

**Saturday, May 30th**

Zac came round. He was wearing those stupid clothes again.

When he'd gone Mum and Dad asked me if I wanted some new trainers for my birthday. "I know they're expensive," said Mum, "but we don't want to hold you back."

I told my parents that new trainers were the very last things I wanted.

Dad said, "Well, when you change your mind ..."

I replied that I never, ever would. And that I would continue to spend all my money on much more important things like computer games and superhero comics. My parents didn't say anything more – just smiled at me in a highly annoying way.

**Tuesday, June 2nd**

Zac is really depressed. His cousin Phil rang him. Phil said that he'd just had an excellent kissing session with his girlfriend.

"He's doing all that," moaned Zac, "and not one girl has even come near me."

I cheered Zac up by reminding him that most girls are bad news. Also, you can't just see them now and again. They make you see them on Friday and Saturday nights. And often during the week as well.

And then there's the cost of a girlfriend. She'll expect you to buy her a present on her birthday, and there'll be Valentine's day too.

Now, if I ever have a girlfriend, I'll meet her in town for just one hour a week. Maybe on her birthday I might take her to McDonald's as well.

But that's really all the time I'm going to spend with her. And I'll never, ever let her come to my house. In fact, I won't even tell her where I live.

You've got to keep some privacy, haven't you?

**Thursday, June 4th**

Zac has bought a skateboard. "I bet the girls come flocking now," he said.

I didn't say anything.

Zac really isn't himself at the moment. But I won't leave him all by himself at this time of crisis.

**Friday, June 5th**

**6 p.m.**

Zac's just asked if I want to go to Watson's Youth Club in town tonight.

To be honest, I don't. But Zac's dead keen to go. He said, "Come on, we'll have a game of pool there. It'll be a laugh."

So I've agreed to meet up with him, even though I'd rather stay here.

**10.15 p.m.**

I'm back. What a weird evening! When Zac met me he was all dressed up. He was *wearing* his skateboard. He posed about with it hanging over one shoulder.

"Looks pretty cool, doesn't it?" he said in a hopeful way.

Outside the youth club there was a boy jumping on and off his skateboard and just showing off. A group of girls stood watching him.

"That's Danny Dyer," whispered Zac to me. "He's won medals for skateboarding."

We watched him for ages, or so it seemed, then we went inside.

Would you believe it? Zac and I never got to play pool, because the tables were broken and the balls were missing. And the cues were all snapped. So we didn't do anything really. We just hung about. I felt as if I was in a huge waiting room.

In the end, Zac went over to this group of older boys from our school. Some had skateboards too. Others stood with their hands hanging down by their sides as if they were apes.

Zac tagged along beside them, laughing loudly whenever they laughed. And I stood alongside Zac in my stripey top, ancient jeans and elderly trainers.

Zac kept giving me funny looks.

"What's wrong?" I asked.

Zac tutted. "You could have made more of an effort. Haven't you got anything else to wear?"

"You know I haven't … anyway, I thought we came here just to play pool."

"We might meet some girls," whispered Zac.

"Oh, you never said that," I replied.

Zac began staring at two girls from our class.

"Isn't she gorgeous?" he murmured.

"Which one?" I asked.

12

"Which one?" he repeated scornfully, as if I'd just said something really stupid. "Jade's OK ... but Emily's just so lush."

I must admit, Emily is quite pretty. She's smallish with long, dark hair and very big eyes.

Then she smiled at us.

"She wants us to go over," whispered Zac eagerly.

We went over.

But Zac just stood there, gazing at Emily in a disgusting, sloppy way. He left me to do all the talking. I chatted to Emily about school. And about the teachers. She was quite chatty. But her friend Jade wasn't. She was too busy looking at Danny Dyer, the skateboard champion.

I asked Jade a question. I was only being polite. But she didn't even bother to answer, just went on making eyes at Danny Dyer.

I think Emily was a bit embarrassed by her friend being so rude. So she asked me, "What would you be doing tonight if you weren't here, Spencer?"

"Oh, playing on my computer," I began.

Suddenly I felt Zac poking me in the ribs. What on earth was wrong? I went on talking to Emily. "Or I might have repaired one of my model aeroplanes."

Zac poked me in the ribs again and hissed down my ear.

"Don't blow it for me … just shut up, now."

So I did. I didn't say another word, neither did Zac.

Shortly afterwards Zac and I walked away.

"Why were you poking me all the time?" I asked.

Zac sighed. "You don't talk to girls about model aeroplanes."

14

"Why not?"

Zac suddenly laughed and patted me on the shoulder.

"Oh, Spencer, you know less about girls than I do."

This thought seemed to cheer him up loads and he laughed again.

Dear diary, I still don't know what I did wrong. I was just giving an honest answer to a question. That's all.

### Saturday, June 6th

Zac's gone off to the youth club again. Only this time he didn't ask me if I wanted to go with him.

Well, I hated last night. And I don't care if I never go there again, but I was a bit hurt that Zac didn't even ask me.

So anyway, I stayed at home tonight and didn't really do much at all.

But I felt dead happy and comfortable.

**Tuesday, June 9th**

Zac's very depressed.  Again!

He wants Emily to be his girlfriend but doesn't think he has a hope.  He asked me what I thought.

Trying to be cheerful, I said, "I don't think it's hopeless, but it is pretty unlikely."

Zac swallowed hard and thanked me for my honesty.

**Thursday, June 11th**

**6.30 p.m.**

Great news!  Zac's just rung me up, sounding happier than he has for weeks.  Then he asked me if I wanted to have a kick about in the park, just like we used to.

I really think things are getting back to normal again.

**9.45 p.m.**

No, they're not. Nothing's normal at all and I've had a totally rotten evening.

I met Zac at the park. He was all dressed up in his new clothes.

"They aren't very good for playing football," I pointed out. He hardly answered. He was too busy patting his hair. He also stank of aftershave and hair gel. Then I noticed he'd brought his skateboard with him.

We started playing football when Emily and Jade turned up. They sat on this seat watching us.

"What are they doing here?" I asked.

"I don't know," said Zac. "Still, we'd better just say hello, hadn't we?"

"I suppose so," I muttered.

Zac almost ran over to them.

17

He stood leaning on the skateboard, as if it was a walking stick.  And every time he looked at Emily I could hear him breathing dead quickly.  Jade did most of the talking.  She was moaning about her parents and how they wouldn't let her get her belly button pierced.

"Why on earth would you want to have that done?" I asked.  "Aren't you aware of the many health risks?"

"You sound just like my dad," snapped Jade.  Zac gave me this really furious glare.

He said, "I think it's really mint you want to have that done."

I wasn't sure what "really mint" meant.  It was not something I'd ever heard Zac say before.  It probably came free with his clothes.

I felt all left out.  I did ask Jade, in a friendly way, if she'd seen *Star Trek: The Next Generation* earlier tonight on the telly.

She replied that she hadn't.

Then I asked her if she'd seen last week's episode.  She said that she hated shows like that and had never watched one in her life.

But how did she know she hated *Star Trek: The Next Generation* if she'd never seen it?

I wanted to ask her that.  But I didn't.

I felt really let down.  I'd been looking forward to a nice game of footie.  Instead, we'd wasted the whole time talking rubbish to girls.

**Friday, June 12th**

Tonight Zac told me he'd known Emily and Jade would be in the park yesterday – he'd invited them. So he'd never intended playing footie with me at all.

I just feel so used!

# Chapter 3
# Spencer the (Un)teenager

**Saturday, June 13th**

**7 p.m.**

Zac's off to that youth club again.

He's got a different life to me now. And I'll just have to accept that.

**10.15 p.m.**

Tonight I was watching this American detective show with Mum and Dad. It was quite good until the detective started kissing the woman – who was also the main murder suspect.

They were at it for ages, too. And they were very noisy. Really slurping away.

In the end my dad started tapping his leg and I could hear Mum shuffling about too. But I didn't look at either of them. I couldn't. I was too embarrassed.

Then they started removing some of their clothes (I mean the man and woman on television, not my mum and dad).

I could feel my parents getting tenser and tenser. And my face was now redder than two beetroots.

Dear diary, watching people snogging on telly with your parents is just about the worst torture in the whole world.

In the end, I managed to croak, "Did you hear how Manchester City got on today, Dad?"

"No, I didn't," he replied.

"They won two-nil.  Arsenal did well too, four-one and ..."

I went on to recite all the football scores I could remember.  By the time I'd finished, the couple on the screen had stopped at last.  And very luckily, the woman in the film got arrested shortly afterwards.

**Monday, June 15th**

Something dead horrible has just happened.

I was sitting in the kitchen, innocently doing my homework, when Dad burst in.  He gave me an odd smile.  I stared at him, alarmed.

"Everything all right, Dad?" I asked.

He nodded, then from behind his back he took out a book.  He put it down on the table.

"We thought you might want to read this ... in your spare time."

I picked it up, then, when I saw what it was, I wrinkled up my nose in total disgust. The book was about the facts of life. You know, how you get babies and all that carry on.

"Have a look inside," urged Dad.

I didn't want to be rude so I flicked open a few pages. The book had some really yucky pictures in it and it was also very long – 173 pages – not counting the index.

"Thanks a lot," I murmured. "But in fact, we did all this in Biology years ago."

"Oh," Dad's voice fell.

Then Mum came in. She had a weird smile on her face too. "We just thought you might find this book helpful."

"After all, you're going to be a teenager soon," said Dad.

They both laughed in a nervous way.

Dear diary, why is everyone making such a big deal out of me turning 13? It's just a number, that's all.

Then Dad said, "Well, there's everything you need to know in that book, but," he added, "if you're worried about anything you can always come and talk to me."

I couldn't think of anything more terrible.

"No, the book's fantastic," I said, trying to sound as cheerful as I could. "Just what I wanted. Thanks a lot."

These days, everyone I know has started turning into a looney. Sometimes I think I'm the only sane person left.

## Wednesday, June 17th

At school, every time Emily walks past, Zac declares, "Just look at her!" Then he makes a sound like a seal asking for a fish. I fear he is in the grip of deep emotions.

## Friday, June 19th

6.45 p.m.

Mum and Dad are off tonight to some boring office party. They said that as I am nearly a teenager they won't make me have a babysitter.

"We think you're old enough to be trusted now."

That's one tiny perk of being a teenager, I suppose.

I mentioned this to Zac. I also said he could pop round later if he wanted. There's a very good (and very bloodthirsty) programme about sharks I taped recently. I thought we could both watch it together. Zac said he would like to do that. He also mentioned that he is getting rather bored of the youth club now. So I was quite happy – until five minutes ago. That's when Zac rang me to say he was still coming round but would it be all right if he brought Emily and Jade with him?

I was dead shocked. When you think you're spending your evening watching sharks and then discover you're entertaining girls instead – well, that takes some getting used to, doesn't it?

But Zac said this was his one big chance to get together with Emily. So I couldn't say no, could I? The three of them are going to be round here in about 15 minutes.

I'll write some more later.

**10.15 p.m.**

Later.

I feel rather pleased with myself. This is what happened.

Zac arrived at seven o'clock with Emily and Jade whispering together. The girls sat on the couch while Zac and his skateboard were on the only chair. I could have squeezed beside Emily and Jade on the couch but thought that might seem a bit pushy.
So instead, I crouched on the floor in a casual manner.

No-one said anything much. In fact, the conversation flowed like cement. Emily and I did most of the chatting. Zac kept jumping up with his skateboard behind his neck. Then he'd lean against the wall, posing all the time. Jade asked him, "What can you do on that skateboard?"

"Oh, loads of things," said Zac.

"Show us then," she demanded.

Zac shook his head sadly. "I'm afraid I've done my ankle in, doing tricks."

"Oh, ha ha," said Jade rudely. "It's freezing in here," she added.

"No it isn't," said Emily.

"Well, I'm cold," Jade muttered.

"Jade'd freeze in a heat wave," smiled Emily.

But I got up and put the heating on. Soon the house was boiling hot. And Jade was still grumbling away. Emily thanked me though. And I noticed she kept glancing at me. I think she was pleased I was such a good host.

Then Jade asked to see my CDs. She rifled through them. "There's not one decent one here," she sighed. "I don't know how you can live in this house, it's so boring."

I was totally fed up with her now. But I didn't let it show. Instead, I said I'd make us all some coffee.

I was in the kitchen for about four seconds when Jade crashed in. "I suppose we ought to leave them alone for a minute," she said. Then she laughed rudely and said what sounded like, "But I can't think why Emily'd be interested in him."

Next Jade opened the fridge. "You've got no pizzas," she cried, in a shocked voice.

"No, sorry."

"And you haven't got any Diet Coke."

"Sorry again."

"I'd starve if I lived in this house." But she still managed to load up a tray with things to eat.

Then Emily came in. "Oh, Jade, you've made yourself at home."

We took all the food back into the sitting room. Jade scoffed most of it, then asked where the loo was. Emily left with her.

"Girls never go to the loo on their own," explained Zac.

"I did know that," I said. "I'm not totally ignorant about what girls do."

They were upstairs for ages.

"What's going on?" hissed Zac. He crept up the stairs. I followed him. "I can hear what they're saying," Zac hissed. "Jade says she's bored and wants to go. But Emily says it'll be rude if they go now."

The bathroom door opened. Zac and I shot back into the sitting room.

"Come on," said Zac to me. "Try and say something interesting. Don't blow this for me."

Talk about stress.

I decided we needed some entertainment.

Now, I realised girls wouldn't be interested in a two hour programme about sharks (you see, I do know quite a bit about girls). So instead, I announced I was putting on a tape which Zac and I had made. It's a video of all the opening bits from TV programmes. And it's dead good. Would you believe, we've got nearly 70 shows on the tape. We haven't just videoed modern shows either. We've got *The Sweeney* from satellite as well. So it's quite a historical video, really.

When I put the tape on Zac looked at me with absolute horror in his eyes. I couldn't think why, as it really livened things up. Even Jade was laughing and enjoying herself.

Then the girls left and Zac walked them home.

Dear diary, I don't want to sound big-headed. But I really think I saved tonight.

I stopped the evening from being a total disaster.

**Saturday, June 20th**

**9.15 p.m**.

You won't believe this. Zac has just stormed out of my house. We've had a massive row.

He was furious with me for playing that tape last night. He said it gave off completely the wrong vibes. And it made us look like a pair of boffins.

"But Jade and Emily were really enjoying themselves."

"No, they weren't," he snapped. "They were laughing because they were so embarrassed."

I stared at him, totally puzzled. "But what's so embarrassing about our tape?"

Zac couldn't say straight away.

"Come on, tell me," I cried.

"Well, it just seems really sad, spending so much time doing that." Then he added, "It was all right before ... but not once you're a teenager."

"Being a teenager ... that's all everyone talks about," I shouted. "And I'm sick of it." Then I added, "You've changed so much lately."

"I had to," cried Zac, "otherwise I'd get left behind like you."

"Oh, thanks a lot."

"I'm sorry, Spencer, but it's the truth. And you're cramping my style."

"Well, those clothes you're wearing don't look right on you ... you look stupid in them," I snapped back at him. Zac shouted back, "At least I'm not a geek like you." Then he marched off.

Never before have Zac and I exchanged such harsh words.

**12.15 a.m.**

I'm still awake. I'm thinking. Zac and I have been friends ever since we met at primary school, seven years ago. I'm not sure if we're friends any more though.

If only Zac hadn't started turning into a teenager. That was when all our problems began.

**Sunday, June 21st**

Zac didn't call me and I never rang him. Spent most of today making a second video of opening credits from TV shows. I don't care who knows either. If turning into a teenager means giving up worthwhile things like this, then I shan't ever be one. I shall just go on being me all through my teens. I won't have anything to do with designer clothes, or girls, or body piercing, or any of it. And I won't worry at all about what people think of me. No, I shall let it all pass me by.

Do you know what I'm going to be?

An (Un)teenager. That's me, dear diary.

Spencer the (Un)teenager.

# Chapter 4

# Zac in a State

**Monday, June 22nd**

I really didn't think Zac would call for me this morning. But he did.

He mumbled, "I think we both said things we shouldn't have on Saturday."

I mumbled back that he was right.

Then we started chatting about other things, which was fine by me.

At the end of school, Zac told me that Emily is still talking to him – even though I showed them our TV video.  He sounded very relieved.  I asked Zac if he'd like a kick-about in the park tonight.  He said he didn't really do that anymore.  He added he was sorry. I said, "Don't worry about it."

And I had a kick-about by myself.

**Tuesday, June 23rd**

Zac said he's going to ask Emily out tomorrow.

**Wednesday, June 24th**

Zac couldn't ask Emily out as he's got a spot.  But when he's got rid of his spot he'll do the deed.

**Friday, June 26th**

Zac's spot had shrunk enough for him to ask Emily out.  And she said ... yes.  They're going to the cinema tomorrow night.  Zac can't believe it.  Neither can I in fact, but I am dead pleased for him.

Saturday, June 27th

4 p.m.

This afternoon I spied my dad prowling around my bedroom. "You haven't got much space in here, have you?" he said. "I just wondered if you'd like to pack your Lego up into the attic."

I was so stunned I could hardly speak. "Why would I want to do that?" I squeaked.

"Well, I just thought you might be a bit old for Lego now," he tried to smile at me, "seeing as you'll be a teenager soon."

I didn't smile back. I merely said in a frosty voice, "The Lego stays exactly where it is, thank you."

And I nearly added, "I have no intention of turning into a teenager either."

**4.30 p.m.**

I've just rung Zac to wish him luck on his date tonight. He was already getting dressed up.

"Do you think I should wear a black shirt?" he asked.

"Yeah, that'll look smart," I replied.

"But dandruff shows up on black and I bet I'll have tons of that tonight," Zac went on.

"Well, perhaps you'd better stick to something lighter then," I said. "And just calm down. Enjoy yourself."

"You're not supposed to enjoy dates," said Zac. "They're like job interviews, really. Anyway ... thanks for calling, but I'd better carry on getting ready."

**7 p.m.**

Zac's date will have started now.

**10.15 p.m.**

Do you suppose it's still going on? Zac's date, I mean. I really do hope it's going all right for him.

**10.20 p.m.**

I wonder if he got a kiss off Emily.

**10.25 p.m.**

I'm only curious, that's all.

**Sunday, June 28th**

**12 p.m.**

Zac's just popped round. He was beaming with relief, so I knew the date with Emily had gone well.

He said it was hard to know what to talk about at first.

"For a bit we were so desperate we even chatted about you," he chuckled. "But then once the film started we relaxed. And at the

41

end of the film," Zac's face was one huge smile now, "we began kissing, dead passionate stuff."

I'm chuffed to bits for him. Only he kept on and on about kissing girls as if he's some kind of expert now and that did get a bit annoying.

**12.15 p.m.**

I suppose most boys in my class have snogged a girl by now. I'm probably one of the very few who hasn't.

I wouldn't mind having a crack at kissing a girl. Just out of interest. But I'm really not that fussed. I mean, I can wait. Girls are such a lot of hassle. Even Emily.

**12.25 p.m.**

Zac's not sure when he should call Emily to fix up another date. He doesn't want to appear too keen.

I suggested next Wednesday but he thinks that's way too long to wait.

**6.50 p.m**.

Zac rang Emily this evening. He's afraid he might have rung her a bit too early, as she seemed very surprised to hear from him. She also said she'd let him know about a second date.

"What do you think that means?" asked Zac. "Have I blown it?"

I said I was sure he hadn't. But girls obviously don't like to be rushed.

I bet he wishes he'd listened to me now and waited until Wednesday.

**Monday, June 29th**

Emily hardly came near Zac at school today. She spent most of the day whispering with Jade. Zac watched all this with a tortured glare.

43

### Tuesday, June 30th

Emily continues to ignore Zac at school. He blames Jade. He says she is turning Emily against him. I'm not sure what I think.

### Wednesday, July 1st

Zac rang Emily three times tonight. The third time he rang, she answered. But she still wasn't sure about going out again. Zac's totally convinced that Jade has made Emily turn against him.

### Thursday, July 2nd

Result! Zac has at last got Emily to go out with him again. He is taking her out for a meal tomorrow. But look what it's doing to his health! He has been stressed out all week.

I'm sorry, dear diary, but I just don't think girls are worth it.

**Friday, July 3rd**

**4.00 p.m.**

Zac's had to buy a new shirt for this meal. And a large, gold chain. He's got enough money for the food – but only if Emily doesn't have a starter. So I've lent him some cash, just in case she's extra hungry. I've been thinking of all the money girls cost you. I reckon dating a girl can cost as much as buying a house.

**8.45 p.m.**

Zac's just called round – and in a right state too.

I couldn't believe my eyes when I saw him. Then he handed me back the money I'd lent him.

"Won't need this after all," he said in solemn tones.

"Didn't she turn up?"

He shook his head. "Left me standing outside the restaurant like a lemon. Then Jade (he spat the word) rang me on my mobile. She just said, 'Emily couldn't make it'.

"When I asked her why, she wouldn't tell me. So I got mad and I shouted, 'This is all your fault. You've turned Emily against me'.

"And she shouted back, 'No, I haven't, it's you ... you can't even kiss properly'.

"I said, 'What do you mean by that?'

"She replied, 'When you kissed Emily you nearly sucked her tongue out. She said it was like being kissed by a Hoover'."

Zac's voice shook as he told me that last thing. Then he hissed, "You won't tell anyone what Jade said ..."

"Of course not," I cried.

"Do you swear?"

"I swear," I said.

And I really wouldn't.

Zac is now a broken man.

**Saturday, July 4th**

Just been round to see Zac. He is still a broken man.

**Sunday, July 5th**

**6 p.m.**

My parents asked if I was sure I wouldn't like a party for my thirteenth birthday. I said I was positive. I just wanted to go to Alton Towers as I had done last year and the year before that ... nothing will be any different this time.

NOTHING!

Then my mum said, why don't I go to Alton Towers and have a party as well? I replied, very slowly, and through gritted teeth, "Mum, I just do not want a party." Then I added, "But if you want to give me an extra treat, I'd appreciate a visit to the tank museum."

### Tuesday, July 7th

I was trying to cheer Zac up so I asked him if he'd like to come to Alton Towers with me. (We'd both gone there last year.) Zac said sadly, "Thanks for the offer, but Alton Towers can have no part in my life now."

### Thursday, July 9th

Zac has now got six zits on his neck. His doomed passion for Emily has caused them to sprout up.

### Saturday, July 11th

My Aunt Lucy came round. "Just one week to go before your birthday, Spencer," she said brightly. Then she added, "Gary (that's her son) vanished before my eyes when he turned 13. Suddenly he was so moody and rude. And he argued with me all the time," she laughed, "but he did start washing himself, so it wasn't all bad."

"Well, I shan't be turning into a teenager in any way at all," I said firmly.

In fact, dear diary, I'm surprised more people don't join me in becoming an (un)teenager. I mean, look at Zac. Before he became a teenager he was pretty happy. Now he's miserable every second of the day. So are most other teenagers. No wonder no-one likes them.

All right, teenagers go to parties. But what happens there? They get dumped, so they drink too much and wake up in a pool of sick. What fun!

Plus, think of all the money I'll save by being an (un)teenager. Plus again, I can keep all my so-called uncool hobbies.

What could be better!

## Tuesday, July 14th

I passed Emily in the shops after school today. I wondered if she knew how she'd messed up Zac's skin. There are nine zits on his neck now and three on his shoulders.

To my huge surprise she started talking to me. She asked when my birthday was. Why, dear diary, does everyone go on and on about that? But I was quite polite and I told her my birthday was just three days away, on Friday, July 17th.

She said, "Well, I hope you have a great day."

That was nice of her, I suppose. I wondered if she was sorry she'd dumped Zac. And should I tell Zac about my little chat with her? I decided against it, as I didn't want to get his hopes up. What would happen if his hopes were dashed again? Then I fear Zac would just go crazy with the pain of it all.

**Thursday, July 16th**

Zac's come round with some amazing news. He's over Emily. These past few weeks he has been racked with love for her. He has also done some stupid things, including following her.

"You mean you've been stalking her," I cried.

Zac sighed heavily and whispered, "Yes."

I had no idea he'd sunk quite that low.

But tonight, while he was gazing longingly at her through the post office window, he decided enough was enough.

"I've let Emily make a fool out of me," he groaned.

"No, you haven't," I quickly replied, "as you were a fool before."

He grinned, then said, "Actually, Spencer, I've found someone else."

I was amazed. "Hey, that was quick."

"It was on my way here. I dropped into McDonald's to get some chips. This girl served me. Really, really pretty. And she smiled at me."

"So what did you do?" I asked.

"Smiled right back at her. I didn't say anything though. Thought I'd play the mystery man this time ... but I'm going to be buying lots of chips from now on."

"Well, it's great you've got over Emily," I said.

"Who?" he asked, then laughed, adding, "Emily's just history now ... she's nothing compared to my new girl. By the way, I'm not going to that stupid youth club any more ... never liked it anyway."

"Didn't you?" I asked.

"No, I was bored out of my skull the whole time. There was never anything to do. All the people who went there ... well, they were just posing about all the time."

Then he asked, "Why did I waste so much of my time there?"

"You were just going through a phase. All teenagers do that ... except me," I added, under my breath.

"I'll tell you something else. I'm useless at skateboarding."

Zac and I both grinned at that. Then he lowered his voice a bit and asked if there was any chance he could go to Alton Towers with me on Sunday after all.

I checked with my dad. And it's all fixed up.

Everything is going back to normal. Just as I wanted.

Can't think of a better way to start my birthday!

# Chapter 5

# The Mystery Birthday Card

Friday, July 17th

7.25 a.m.

MY BIRTHDAY!

Been awake for a full 20 minutes and I don't feel any different at all.

Just wanted you to know that.

**7.45 a.m.**

Opened my presents. Then my parents said they'd bought me an extra one. I was

dead excited – until I saw what it was.
A gold-plated bracelet with my name on it.
Wow!

"We wanted to mark this special day in some way," said Mum.

So they've given me something I can't play with or eat.  I mean, what's the point of it?

But, for their sakes, I tried my very best to look pleased.

**4 p.m.**

Got back from school to find a birthday card waiting for me.  It was a very brightly coloured card, with streamers and people dancing and "Happy Birthday" in gold letters. Then I opened it up and found there was no name inside.  There was just a question mark and a rather badly drawn heart in the corner. *That's a bit strange*, I thought.

**4.30 p.m.**

Just phoned Zac and told him about my card. He said I must have a secret admirer. We both nearly killed ourselves laughing after that. Then he said he's coming round to see my card.

**5.25 p.m.**

I can't believe what's just happened. It's incredible! I still can't take it in.

Zac came round, looked at the card – and I waited for him to start laughing again. But he didn't. He just kept on staring at the card. Then he said, very slowly, "I have seen this card before. I saw Emily buying it in the post office on Wednesday afternoon."

"You're joking," I gasped.

Zac shook his head very grimly. He turned all serious.

And I was so amazed I couldn't speak at first.

Why on earth would Emily send me a birthday card and not sign it? And draw a heart on it?

It didn't make any sense. Unless ...

"Well, she must have sent it as a joke," I cried.

"No, I don't think so," said Zac. "You know, she was always asking about you."

"Was she?"

"Yeah, now I think of it, we always seemed to end up talking about you ... Well, what are you going to do about it?"

"You mean you don't mind?"

"After the things she said about me? No, I'm totally finished with her. Besides, I've got my new girl ... I bought some more chips today and we've started talking now ... Do you like Emily, then?"

I felt myself blushing. "She's all right."

Zac laughed. "When are you going to go round to her house then?"

But I could never do that.

**5.35 p.m.**

Could I?

**5.36 p.m.**

No, not ever.

**6.30 p.m.**

Just finished my birthday tea. All I can think about is that stupid card.

**6.35 p.m.**

I can't go on like this. It's time to take firm action.

**7.00 p.m.**

I really wanted to take firm action, to do something now about that card but I ended up doing nothing at all. Well, I just couldn't go up to Emily and ask her if she'd sent me the card. It was probably some kind of sick joke anyway. Maybe Jade told her to do it. Yeah, that's possible, isn't it? Perhaps they're both waiting to see what I'll do next. Well, I'll fool them – I shan't do anything.

**7.30 p.m.**

Rang up Zac. Told him that card had shot my nerves to pieces. What I need is a nice, relaxing game of footie. We're going to meet in the park in 15 minutes.

# Chapter 6
# "It's Started!"

**8.30 p.m.**

You won't believe what's just happened. But everything I'm telling you is true.

I went off to the park and was kicking a football about waiting for Zac. Only he never turned up. Instead – and this was so weird – Emily popped up.

She just appeared in the park. And she stood smiling at me. I walked over to her. I was so shocked to see her my legs wobbled a bit.

"Happy birthday," she said.

"Thanks." My voice was wobbling a bit too.

Emily said, "Zac told me you wanted to see me."

I jumped. "Zac did what?"

"He said you wanted to see me."

"Oh – what else did he say?"

"Not much, he just said you were waiting in the park for me and then he put the phone down ... Are you waiting for me?"

"Not exactly."

"Oh." Emily stared at the ground. "Just Zac messing about, was it?" She made as if to go away. But then she turned round again. "I never said those things about Zac that Jade said, you know. I just mentioned in confidence to her that he wasn't a great kisser – and Jade made the rest up. I was so angry with her. Well, we're not even talking now." She stopped. "See you then."

That's when I piped up, "Did you send me a birthday card?"

"No law against it, is there?"

"No, I was just a bit surprised."

"It's no big deal. It's just you're different from the others and I like that."

She was smiling right at me now. Smiling in a way no-one's ever smiled at me before. I got this funny, tingling feeling all over my body. And the next thing that happened was ... I kissed her on the cheek. I thought she might object. But she seemed quite pleased by my action.

Meanwhile, I was wondering what to do with my hands. They were both hanging by my sides as if I were a penguin.

Suddenly, I put my arms around her waist and we had another much longer kiss. And it was good ... in fact, quite refreshing, really.

We were both a bit out of breath when we'd finished. Then we heard this laughing behind us and we realised we'd been watched by a group of boys. We were both embarrassed now. So I just said, "Thanks very much for that. Goodnight."

"Goodnight," said Emily.

And that brought an end to the evening's weird events.

Feel totally confused now, but also quite content.

**9.05 p.m.**

I am content no longer. I've just done something that is truly worrying. Sorry, dear diary, but I don't feel I can even write about it, yet. I'm too ashamed.

**9.45 p.m.**

It's no good. I can't keep my guilty secret anymore. Prepare to be totally shocked.

It was about nine o'clock. I'd just finished writing the last entry in my diary. Then I looked at my birthday card from Emily again and at the heart, which now I saw was really quite well drawn. The next thing I knew I was glancing at my smelly trainers and ... wondering how much new ones would cost. Oh, the shame of it! Afterwards I was so angry with myself.

Could this be the first sign that I'm on the turn? Are my days as an (un)teenager numbered? Or was it just a little blip? I have to tell you, two minutes ago I caught myself staring at my trainers for a second time and wondering once more about new ones ... but you can guess the rest.

Then I went over and looked at my face in the mirror.

Of course, I've done that before. But this time it was as if I was studying myself. And I began noticing every little spot.

**It's starting, isn't it?**

I'm becoming the thing I most dreaded. A TEENAGER.

No doubt more signs will occur shortly. Any day now I'll start deciding whether I'm going to be a skater or a goth. And I'll go out and buy all the stupid, baggy clothes. I'll get depressed all the time and moody. The only thing I'll think about is how I look and acting cool. Dear diary, can I still save myself from this terrible future? Or is it too late?

**10.15 p.m.**

There should be a help-line or someone you can ring. I'm turning into a teenager and I need to know how to stop it.

**10.30 p.m.**

When I wake up in the morning will more changes have taken place? I don't think I'll sleep a wink tonight.

**10.40 p.m.**

Just thought of something. Emily likes me already, doesn't she? She said I was "different from the others". So I don't need to turn into someone else to impress her. All right, I could smarten myself up a little bit.

And it wouldn't kill me to get some new trainers.

But I'll be a teenager on my own terms. No-one else will tell me what clothes to get – or what hobbies I'm allowed. I'll still like model aeroplanes and tank museums and programmes about sharks.

I'll still go on being me. I won't get all worked up about what I look like or any of that.

So that's what I'm going to do. Wish me luck, won't you?

**11.20 p.m.**

Dear diary, just one last thing to confess. Something I didn't write down before. When I kissed Emily, it wasn't just good and quite refreshing, which is what I wrote back then. No, it was much, much better than that. And afterwards I felt so happy. The kind of happiness when you feel you can do anything you want.

I thought I should put that into my diary.

**11.30 p.m.**

But I'm still an (un)teenager. Only with better trainers. And maybe a new hairstyle as well. Well, maybe ...

Barrington Stoke would like to thank all its readers for commenting on the manuscript before publication and in particular:

Natasha Blood
Mrs A. Brown
Alice Crane
Lucy Edwardes
Neil Evans
Kate Forrester
Elizabeth Harvey
Jamie Hodgson
Jan Huxon
Laura Hyatt
Haroon Khan
Fergus MacKie
Sue Morris
Josephine Owen

Bob Parker
Stephanie Penman
Annabel Pitt
Rebecca Roberts
Brett Sabel
Robyn Saddler
Paul Scott
Mrs S. Scott
Martin Searle
Jessica Smyth
Ben Soep
Claire Vardy
Mrs Whiteley

## Become a Consultant!

Would you like to give us feedback on our titles before they are published?  Contact us at the email address below – we'd love to hear from you!

info@barringtonstoke.co.uk
www.barringtonstoke.co.uk